HEAR O ISRAEL

To my husband, Robert Clark Treseder,
and our children, Michael and Gloria

Hear O Israel

A Story of the Warsaw Ghetto

by Terry Walton Treseder
illustrated by Lloyd Bloom

Atheneum 1990 New York

Atheneum
Macmillan Publishing Company
866 Third Avenue, New York, NY 10022
Collier Macmillan Canada, Inc.
First Edition
Designed by Nancy B. Williams
Printed in the United States of America
10 9 8 7 6 5 4 3 2 1

Library of Congress Cataloging-in-Publication Data
Treseder, Terry W. (Terry Walton)
Hear o Israel: a story of the Warsaw Ghetto/by Terry Walton
Treseder; illustrated by Lloyd Bloom.—1st ed. p. cm.
Summary: A Jewish boy describes life in the Warsaw Ghetto and his
family's ultimate transference to and decimation in the camp of
Treblinka.
ISBN 0-689-31456-6
1. Holocaust, Jewish (1939-1945)—Poland—Juvenile fiction.
2. Concentration camps—Poland—Fiction. [1. Jews—Poland—
Warsaw—Persecution—Fiction. 2. World War, 1939-1945—Jews—
Fiction. 3. Holocaust, Jewish (1939-1945)—Poland—Fiction.
4. Treblinka (Poland: Concentration camp)—Fiction.]
I. Bloom, Lloyd, ill.
II. Title.
PZ7.T7317He 1990 [Fic]—dc19
89-7029 CIP AC

CONTENTS

BAR MITZVAH

My foot standeth in an even place:
in the congregation will I bless the Lord.
—Psalms 26:12

MY BROTHER BECAME A MAN THREE YEARS AGO.

I sat in the congregation with Uncle Adam and my cousins Joseph, Abe, and Jacob, while Simon stood on the platform beside Papa to read his portion of the Torah.

Mama sat in the balcony behind us with my sister, Rachel, and Baby Benjamin.

I looked up to see Mama's face. Her eyes were wet with pride.

Simon looked grown, draped in his new woolen tallith and crowned with a tefillin over his forehead.

I knew that inside the little leather tefillin box were carefully written portions of holy scripture. I knew that Simon had another tefillin bound to his left arm.

I remembered the commandment from the Torah to bind our minds and bodies to the words of God. "Bind them as a sign on your hand, let them serve as frontlets between your eyes."

Simon held a slender stick made of silver and shaped like a pointing hand. Moving it lightly across

the Hebrew scroll, he recited the whole week's selection by himself!

Papa was proud.

As blessings were said and prayers uttered, I felt safe.

Yet, I should have been afraid. I could see the cracks in the windows where rocks had been thrown. I could see the black, sooty splotches on the wall where fires had been lighted. I could see barrenness in a room robbed of its handsome candlesticks, velvet curtains, and silver goblets.

The people of the city hated us. And the soldiers who marched into Warsaw not long ago hated us more.

When the soldiers came, Papa shrugged his shoulders. "Strangers from here, strangers from there. It makes no difference."

But the pictures posted on the buildings frightened me. I knew they were pictures of Jews. Only we Jews wore long black coats and curls on either side of our faces. The pictures looked like snarling dogs biting at women and children. Some were fat Jews sitting on piles of money. The worst were the pigs dressed like Jews, all snorting wickedly. We are forbidden to eat pigs' flesh because we believe they are unclean animals. To be a pig is to be the lowest of creatures.

A gang of boys once caught me going home from synagogue school.

"Take a piece of pork, stick it on a fork, and give it to the curly headed Jew, Jew, Jew!"

They wrestled me to the ground and took out a pair of scissors.

"Let's cut the curls off this pig!" they shouted.

I cried and kicked and punched. But it was no use. They cut off my curls, tore my coat, and beat me about the face. At last I managed to escape and run away. I ran so fast and so hard that my chest hurt and my legs buckled. I never looked back until I stumbled up the stairs to my home. I could not stop sobbing from shame.

"You were lucky," Mama said as she patted my bruises with ice. "If a soldier had been nearby, it would have been very bad."

Though Mama kept us inside the apartment except for synagogue worship and school, we heard of terrible happenings. Houses were burned, windows smashed, Jews killed and wounded. In the middle of the night we could hear distant gunshots and screams.

Simon said the soldiers told the people to get rid of the Jews.

"How can they believe these stories?" Simon asked Papa during supper one day. "They say lies about us. They say we kill Christian babies during Passover, hide gold in our pockets, and plot to keep them poor. None of it is true. Can't they see we are as poor as they are?"

Papa looked at Simon with much patience. "These stories—" He waved his hand as though he would make them disappear. "They are not new. They are as old as Babylon. The townsman blames the Jew because he is poor. He blames the Jew because he has no one else to blame. Shalom, my son, shalom. Peace and patience. Our people will survive."

The streets became dangerous. Elders walked the children to synagogue school. Women went to market in large groups. No one left home at night. Even so, we were shouted at, spat upon, pelted with rotten lettuce, pieces of glass, even bricks.

Why did they hate us so?

But I felt safe in the synagogue.

All the people I loved were close around me. My uncles, my cousins, my grandparents, my friends. We were like chicks nestled snugly under the warm body of God.

> "The Lord will give strength
> unto His people; the Lord will bless
> His people with peace."

We mingled amid congratulations while Mama hurried home to prepare Simon's bar mitzvah celebration.

"Shalom aleichem!"

"Congratulations!"

"Your brother is a good scholar!"

I said to myself, "I will study the Torah. I will learn the holy Hebrew language. Then I will be a man like my brother, Simon. He will be proud at my bar mitzvah."

HUNGER

I have eaten ashes like bread,
and mingled my drink with weeping.

— *Psalms 101:9*

MAMA LOOKED BEAUTIFUL ON THE SABBATH.

Every day but Sabbath, Mama had wrinkles on her face. She was busy, always busy scrubbing, washing, cooking, ironing, shopping, scolding. She moved hurriedly, worried about yeast for bread, diapers for Benjamin, pennies for candles.

But every Friday before nightfall, as Mama covered her head with her white lace shawl and lighted the Sabbath candles, she drew heaven into her face. There were no wrinkles on Mama's face.

Rachel and Benjamin would cling to Mama's skirt and stare up at "Angel-Mama" with wonder. Shielding her eyes from the candlelight, she murmured blessings on us.

"May my sons learn to love God. May they learn to love His holy words. May my daughter be like Sarah, a comfort to her husband, a mother of Israel. May my children grow up strong. May they be safe from evil in body and soul."

We knew that the Holy One heard Mama's prayer. We felt so much love around us.

Mama set the table with her best dishes and placed flowers in the center. Proudly she invited family to come to Sabbath supper. Grandma and Grandpa Rothenberg lived with us now, because they could no longer pay their rent. Uncle Adam ate with us too, because he was not yet married. He was an important man now. The soldiers had made him president of the Jewish Commission.

Food was hard to find since they had built the wall around our part of the city. Still, Mama managed to save enough money during the week to make two loaves of challah bread and kreplach stew. I liked to fish out the bits of chicken hidden inside the fried pastry. It was truly a feast for the Sabbath!

I was glad the soldiers had built the wall. We saw no more gangs looking for Jews to hurt. We saw only silent soldiers everywhere.

But Simon was angry. "We are living in a ghetto now, a prison!"

Papa shook his head mildly and pointed his finger in the air. "A Jewish ghetto, Simon. They shut us in, it is true. But then we shut them out. And we have our own government now. Think of that! We eat with the first Jewish president in Warsaw." He nodded his head proudly at Uncle Adam.

Uncle Adam was not old. He had just finished law school. Everyone liked Uncle Adam. The men liked him because he was serious and scholarly. The women liked him because he was good for their daughters to marry.

"What can the Jewish Commission really do?" Simon asked boldly.

Adam folded his hands in front of him and looked at Simon. He never said very much. He spent much time pondering. "The soldiers decide how much food comes into our town and patrol the streets. The Jewish Commission will take care of all the other details of government. We will ration out the food, run the orphanage, synagogue school, and other public functions."

"We seem to have more freedom than we did before," Grandpa agreed. "I remember when Jews were driven out of the city entirely. We are very lucky."

"Yes, very lucky indeed." Papa lifted his wineglass. "Praise be to God for our blessings."

But every day I wondered if we were so lucky. People became poorer and poorer. Soon there was not enough food for everyone. We began to eat two meals a day, then one. No meat could be found in the ghetto, only onions and a little flour.

Grandpa and Grandma often gave their supper to Rachel or Benjamin because they cried so much for food.

I did not cry. I was trying to be a man. But my belly hurt when I went to school. My friends looked hungry too. They began to look like old men. Some even coughed and hobbled like old men.

People around us began to die from hunger. I saw Uncle Mordecai's whole family buried with many other people in one big grave.

Grandpa fell and died on the street as we walked to worship one morning. There were no soldiers to see us, so we quickly carried him to the cemetery and found a little place to bury him.

I cried when Mama died. She died giving birth to my baby sister. The little baby did not live long because we had no milk.

Everyone seemed to get sick. Papa called it typhus.

"Isaac," Rachel whispered to me one night. "Are we going to die?"

"I don't know," I answered.

"Typhus seems better than starving, don't you think? It doesn't take so long."

When little Benjamin got sick, Rachel cared for him. They both died from typhus.

Papa never smiled anymore. His eyes were red and sad. He prayed all the time. I knew, because when he thought I was sleeping, he would clinch his hands together and speak to the ceiling, staring and staring.

Grandma lighted our one Sabbath candle. But she did not look like an angel. Her cheeks were sunken and her eyes blank.

The past year had been very bad. The streets were piled with people who had died from typhus and hunger. No one had enough money to pay burial taxes. No one was strong enough to bury the bodies. Many sick and starving people huddled in the snow because they had no money. It was hard to walk through the crowded, smelly streets to synagogue school, for I felt weak and sleepy. I wanted to sit down and close my eyes and never open them again.

Only a few boys were left in school. We had another new teacher. He used to be a butcher, but he knew a little Hebrew.

Simon did not come home very much. He talked of fighting. He joined the other young men who wanted to escape and fight the soldiers. We buried many young men who were shot when they tried to leave the ghetto. I was afraid for my brother.

"Fighting will only bring death to all our people," Papa told Simon sternly. "We must wait for God and endure."

"They are killing us already," Simon scowled angrily. "We mill around like goats in a pen waiting to be butchered."

"Enough!" Papa waved his hand impatiently. "You think only of yourself. A young man has a chance to fight and live. But when the soldiers come in with machine guns, what will the old people do? What will the small children do? What will the tiny babies do? Have you no thought for Uncle Adam's orphans?"

"The old people and children and babies and orphans are dying even now," Simon challenged Papa. "What will Uncle Adam do when there are no more Jews left for him to govern?"

Poor Uncle Adam tried to be fair. But there was not enough food or money to give away. He told us to keep living our lives. We must go to school, celebrate the High Holy Days.

Purim, the children's festival, came in spring. Papa, Uncle Adam, and other men read the story of Esther. Young men like Simon worked their puppets and pretended to be beautiful Esther and her uncle, Mordecai, who saved the Jews in Persia from wicked Haman. The puppet Haman looked funny with his tall, pointed hat, green face, and frog eyes.

I laughed so hard I forgot the hunger. Banging my pot and booing and cheering made me feel happy again. Uncle Adam was very wise.

This past Passover meal was sad. Not only did we set a cup at the table for Elijah, as we did every year, but for Mama and Grandpa and Rachel and Benjamin as well. We even had a high chair set for Baby Ruthie, who never tasted food.

Instead of an egg, a shank of meat, and bitter herbs, Papa filled the seder plate with a stone, a stick, and a handful of dirt. Papa said we do not need a feast to remember God delivered His people from slavery in Egypt.

Simon was not there. He told Papa we need a living redeemer, not a dead one.

Tradition says the door must be opened for Elijah. But when I opened the door, I saw sick people living in the stairwell. These were the people who could not pay their rent.

"Like sheep they are laid in the grave; death
shall feed on them, and their beauty
shall consume in the grave from their dwelling."

My heart beat with fear.

Then I remembered Mama saying, "But God will redeem my soul from the power of the grave; for He shall receive me. Be not thou afraid."

I could feel Mama's love and was not afraid.

TRAIN RIDE

They that carried us away captive required of us a song.

—*Psalms 142:7*

I ALWAYS WANTED TO RIDE A TRAIN.

But there was never anyplace to go or money to buy a ticket.

Now we were going to leave Warsaw on a train. Papa said the soldiers were taking all the Jews to the east country to work.

"Does that mean we shall eat?" I asked.

"Can a starved mule pull potato carts?" Papa smiled with his mouth, but not with his eyes.

I cupped my hands to Grandma Rothenberg's ear and shouted, "Grandma! We are going on a train ride! We are going to eat again!"

Grandma did not say anything. She only sat and stared through the walls. When Grandma first began to sit like a doll, I was frightened. But Papa told me she was visiting Grandpa and Rachel and Benjamin and Mama. Then I was glad for Grandma. I wished I could visit them too. Especially Mama.

The first train full of Jews had left already. Today it was our turn. Papa and I began to pack our things into boxes.

21

"These things are for you." Papa carried a drawer to my bed. He took out his neatly folded tallith and put it over my head. The tassels hanging from the four corners of the tallith felt like fingers touching my legs.

"You will be a man in three days," Papa said, putting his arm around my shoulder. "I do not know if we can have a bar mitzvah like your brother Simon's."

I nodded my head. I understood. I was happy that Papa remembered. I had not said anything about my bar mitzvah this year because he seemed too sad to remember.

Papa took out his black Sabbath hat and put it on my head. Then he showed me how to wrap the straps of his tefillin around my arm. He took the hat off and wrapped another tefillin around my head. The old box rested heavily on my forehead. The straps felt like Papa's big hands pressed around my head. Papa unwrapped the arm tefillin and wrapped it again. He stepped back and looked at me. We faced each other for some time. Papa's eyes were wet with pride. It was hard not to cry, for I was proud and happy.

"These things should go to Simon," I said.

"Simon does not want them."

"Is it right for a man to cry?" I asked. I felt ashamed because I could not keep from crying.

"There is a time for everything," Papa said. He cried too. He hugged me for a long time.

Last, he gave me his prayer book, the fine little leather book that he always carried with him. Together we read from the morning service:

"Save thy people, and bless thine inheritance, and sustain them forevermore. Our soul doth wait for the Eternal! who is our help and shield. For in Him our heart rejoiceth; for in His sacred name we trust. Then let thy tender mercy, O Eternal, be upon us, even as we have trustingly looked up to thee."

I carefully packed my new treasures in my box.

Suddenly we heard Simon's voice shouting to us as he ran up the stairs, "Papa! Papa! Isaac! Isaac!" He banged open the door and rushed at us. "Papa! Isaac! You must not go! Do not get on that train!"

Papa and I looked at each other. What did Simon mean?

Simon grabbed our arms so tightly it hurt. His face looked wild. "Uncle Adam...Uncle Adam..."

"What did Uncle Adam say?" Papa asked, alarmed.

"He killed himself, Papa! He killed himself!"

Papa looked amazed. He shook his head. "No, no. Not Adam. He is the sensible one."

"Papa, he killed himself yesterday after the train left. Somebody heard him whisper, 'Not even the orphans.'"

"'Not even the orphans'?" Papa looked confused. "So what does that mean? Adam says, 'Not even the orphans,' and kills himself. What does this mean?"

Simon looked impatient and angry. "It means the soldiers are not taking the Jews to work camps. They are taking us to those death camps Caleb told me about."

Papa became angry. "There you go on about Caleb's stories again. Death camps! If they want to kill us, why not shoot us in Warsaw and save a train ride?"

"I don't know, Papa." Simon looked frightened. "But Caleb is not the only one who talks of such things. The soldiers want to kill all the Jews."

Papa waved his hand in the air. "Such talk is non-sense. They are throwing the Jews out of the town, as strangers have been doing for a thousand years. Grandpa Rothenberg was a boy when his family was forced to leave his village. Was he sent to a death camp because he was too small to work? No." Papa pointed his finger in the air. "This is our deliverance, Simon. We shall start a new life in a new place, where it will be safe to live."

Simon did not look so frightened. "Caleb says we should stay here and fight."

"And die?" Papa waved his hands again. "Nonsense."

"Are we really going to work...and eat?" Simon asked hopefully.

"I believe that life will be better out of Warsaw than inside Warsaw."

Simon stared at Papa. Then they hugged each other.

When we came to the train station, it was very noisy. The big black train snorted steam like some angry beast. People shouted at each other.

"Mama! Over here!"

"Get back behind the line!"

"Where is my bag?"

"Are we next?"

The soldiers were everywhere. They pushed people around and shouted orders.

"Old people first! Hurry! Hurry!"

A big soldier took Grandma's arm and pulled her out of the crowd.

"Wait!" Papa pushed his way to the soldier. "She is helpless. She must stay with us."

"Get back!" the soldier shouted. He pushed Papa away.

Simon tried to pull Grandma back with us.

"Get back!" the soldier shouted again, and he pointed his rifle at Simon.

Papa pulled Simon back.

"She will die by herself!" Simon shouted angrily.

"We will find her when the train stops," Papa said. He looked worried.

The old people were put into the train.

"Men next!" the soldiers shouted.

We pushed our way to the train. Women clung to their husbands and cried. Men hugged their children before waving good-bye. Papa and Simon pulled themselves into a boxcar.

"Wait!" A big hand squeezed my shoulder. "You must wait and get on with the women and children."

I looked up at the stern, hard face. It was the same color as his gray helmet.

"He looks younger than he is!" Simon shouted. "He's fifteen years old!"

The soldier scowled. "Get up, then! Quick! Hurry!" He pushed me toward the boxcar.

Simon took my box while Papa took my hand and

pulled me up. We pressed against other men toward the back of the car. More and more men crowded around us until there was little room left to breathe. Tighter and tighter we packed against each other. I could see nothing but black coats about me. My box pressed hard against my ribs.

There was much shouting and noise.

"They are putting the women and children in," Papa said. He had one arm around my shoulder.

Suddenly we heard the women screaming and crying. The sound frightened me.

"What's going on, Papa?" Simon yelled. "I can't see!"

Papa strained his neck. His face turned red with anger. "The soldiers are throwing the small children into the boxcar on top of the women."

Finally, the great steel doors of the boxcar closed. Suddenly it was dark and quiet.

This was not the kind of train ride I had looked forward to. There was no room to sit or move, and so my legs hurt. Sometimes I would squat to sleep, but I was afraid that someone would step on me. The smell in the boxcar became terrible, as there was no place to go to the toilet. The old people in back of us moaned. The women and children in front of us cried. The worst was the thirst. Hunger is very bad. But thirst is more terrible. My throat tightened up. My lips felt chapped and flaky. My mouth ached for water.

The little children cried for water. I wanted to cry, but I did not. I was going to be a man.

The train bumped on and on. It was always dark, so I did not know how long we rode the train. But we stopped several times. Each time it stopped we all fell down upon each other. People yelled and struggled to stand up.

When the soldiers opened the doors, we begged for water. But we did not get water. They took out the bodies of people who had died and put more people inside the car.

Papa and I prayed together often. I was glad for the prayers. They helped me be a man and forget the terrible thirst. I could think about the Holy One, and about Mama, who seemed closer and closer to me every hour.

Simon would not say any prayers. He stood silently, angrily. His face began to look like the soldier's with the gray helmet.

It was a long train ride. But it ended. This time when the train stopped and the doors opened, the soldiers shouted, "Get out! Hurry! Hurry! Get out!"

TREBLINKA

They have said, Come, and let us cut them off from being a nation; that the name of Israel may be no more in remembrance.

—*Psalms 83:4*

"HURRY! HURRY! GET OUT! GET OUT!"

Papa held my hand tightly as we pushed toward the door. The box under my other arm seemed too heavy. I almost left it behind. But I remembered the treasures inside and held it close to me.

We stepped out of the car and stumbled down a ramp. At first I was blinded by sunshine. It hurt my eyes. The hard end of a rifle poked my back.

"Out! Out! Hurry! Hurry!"

Papa and Simon half carried me between two lines of soldiers who pointed rifles at us. When my eyes stopped hurting, I looked around and wondered at the color about me. The sky was a beautiful blue! The trees and grass were healthy green. They did not look thirsty.

"Everything on that pile!"

The soldiers made us throw our boxes and bags onto a large pile. I did not want to give up my treasures.

"We will give them back to you after delousing!" the soldiers shouted.

"What does 'delousing' mean?" I asked Papa.

"They will spray us to kill the lice on our bodies," Papa said tiredly.

I had been too thirsty and tired in the train to notice the lice. But now I felt the crawling, itching bugs that hurt my skin. Suddenly I wanted to get deloused right away. I carefully laid my box on the pile, and the soldiers began to throw our belongings into trucks.

They put the old people in a truck and drove away. I did not see Grandma. Most of the old people had died in the train. Many bodies were put in trucks and taken into the forest. The soldiers pushed the rest of us toward the trucks, separating the women and children from the men.

"You!" A soldier pulled Simon out of line.

Simon looked frightened.

"You will be on the work detail!"

They pushed Simon and other young men into a truck and drove quickly away.

"What are they going to do with Simon?" I asked Papa.

"I think he will be working right away," Papa said, unsure. "They have taken the strongest young men, perhaps to do a special job."

We climbed into a truck.

I held on to the side of the truck as it bumped along the road toward a large camp surrounded by high fences of barbed wire. I could see tall, dark towers and buildings inside the fences.

"What is that?" I asked Papa, pointing to the camp.

Papa did not know.

"Treblinka." A tall man who looked like Uncle Adam smiled kindly at me. "I speak many languages, so I understand what the soldiers say to each other. They are taking us to Treblinka."

"Treblinka." I said the name to feel its sound. I liked the name, but I did not like the ugly camp. "Papa, where is Treblinka?"

Papa did not know.

The tall man did not know either.

It was strange not to know where we were. Perhaps we were on the other side of the world. Maybe the people here did not know about Jews. Maybe the people wouldn't hate us. Perhaps they would give us water to drink and food to eat.

The large line of trucks ahead of us passed through the gates and drove out of sight among the buildings.

The guard at the gate stopped our truck. The driver and the guard began to argue with each other, waving their arms toward the buildings where the other trucks had disappeared.

"What are they saying?" Papa asked the tall man.

"It is hard to hear them over the engine, but it seems they don't have room for us at the delousing station." The tall man listened carefully to the soldiers. "Too many people...one station broken... must wait...behind schedule. The driver wants to know where to put us."

The soldiers stopped shouting; then the guard waved our truck through.

"They must delouse us before the next trainload of people comes in tomorrow." The tall man smiled. "Soldiers like to be efficient."

As we drove through camp, I saw many soldiers. They were everywhere—in the towers, on the roads, around the buildings. But I did not see any other people.

"Where are the other Jews, Papa?" I asked.

Papa did not know. The tall man did not know.

I wondered where the first trainload of Jews had gone. Perhaps they were going to another camp.

They put us in a fenced yard and told us that we would have to wait until tomorrow to be deloused. I was disappointed. It would feel wonderful to be clean and free from bugs again.

The trucks of women and children were taken to another field.

The ground was hard and cold. But I was glad to lie

down after days of standing in a moving train. Papa put his arm around me so that I could rest my head on his shoulder. The soldiers did not like to hear us talking and would shout angrily when they heard whispering.

We were too thirsty to talk, anyway. By now my tongue had swollen until it filled my mouth, and my throat felt covered with painful lumps. It hurt to swallow. Lice bit into me and filth gritted my skull.

But it felt good to be in the clean, open air again, to see the bright stars and moon. A great joy, almost a prayer, filled my heart, for God seemed big and grand in the wide, deep space above.

I woke the next morning when the soldiers began to shout. I sat up and rubbed my eyes and neck. There were sore spots on my back where hard lumps in the ground had poked me throughout the night. Papa helped me stand up, and we hurried to where the soldiers pushed us, to trucks waiting nearby.

The trucks jolted through the camp until we came to a large pit surrounded by high bushes. They herded us into the pit. I could see a long, narrow path leading out of the pit. But I could not see where it led.

The soldiers shouted at us, "Get out! Hurry! Hurry!" They began to beat us on the heads with their rifles. "Get undressed! Hurry!"

We began to undress as quickly as we could. I was

untying my shoes when I looked up and saw Simon. He was wearing a blue armband and staring at me with huge, wild eyes. Nervously he looked around and quickly gave me a crumpled piece of paper. Then he staggered away, picking up piles of clothes. He looked back at me one last time and his face frightened me.

I found Papa and gave him the paper. He read it, then ate it so the soldiers would not find it.

They were taking groups of men up the lane. We could hear the women and children getting out of trucks behind us. They were crying and screaming.

Papa kneeled down in front of me and held my shoulders. "Listen to me, Isaac. We haven't much time." His eyes looked hopeless and sad. "We are not going to be deloused. They are going to kill us."

"Is that what Simon wrote?" I asked, trying hard not to feel afraid.

Papa breathed hard and choked. "He is mad with horror, Isaac. He only wrote of death. 'We all die. No hope. No God.'"

A terrible, roaring hammer seemed to pound at my ears. My heart beat wildly to escape, to run away.

Papa bowed his head and silently wept. His naked shoulders shook in sobs.

I held Papa's knuckles tightly. "Papa, are you afraid?" I felt panic racing to my feet.

Papa looked up, his eyes filled with sorrow. "Your brother Simon has lost his faith."

I thought about what that meant. Simon did not believe in God anymore. He had denied the Holy One in his letter. "Why?" I asked, wondering what could turn my brother against his God.

"I believe he blames God for the cruelty and death he sees."

I could not understand. "But God is not killing us, Papa. The soldiers are killing us."

"Tell me you believe, Isaac," Papa begged with a whisper.

"Papa, I believe." I tried not to cry. "But, Papa, where are we going?"

Papa pointed to the blue sky above. "We are going to heaven, Isaac. Today we shall see Mama again."

"And Rachel?"

"And Benjamin, and Grandpa and Grandma..."

"And Ruthie..."

"And Uncle Mordecai..."

"And Uncle Adam." I thought a moment. "Shall I have my bar mitzvah in heaven, Papa?"

Papa smiled tearfully, nodding his head. He hugged me tightly.

A soldier began to beat us. "Hurry! Hurry! Move!"

Papa stood up. He looked strong again. He took

my hand and walked firmly forward. He began to murmur the ancient words of the Torah that every Jew knows by heart. I repeated the words after him. Soon other voices murmured the prayer with Papa as we walked forward.

> "Hear O Israel: The Lord our God, the Lord is One.
> "Hear O Israel: The Lord our God, the Lord is One."

I knew as I looked around at the faces about me that they knew. They all knew they were going to die. Some faces were old, some very young, like me. They all looked frightened, but brave. They were men. I felt proud to be a man among them.

12

The ceremony was a way of feeling and Joe felt it and felt good.

It was good to see David sitting there. Joe had expected to see a dumb grin on his brother's face but it wasn't there. Something was wrong on David's face. Joe tried to read it and couldn't. He tried to think of something else. I'm just sitting up here faking it, Davey. This kind of stuff is your stick, he thought.

Aunt Lou was there watching David. If she can't figure what's wrong, Joe thought, I sure as hell can't.

Ellie was there but her huge ponytail was gone. Her hair had been cut into a super-high and beautiful natural. Over and over, Joe saw the bright flashes of light from her camera. She stumbled once trying to take his picture.

Phil was there, sitting next to Ellie.

The only people missing are Pop and Momma and Paul, Joe thought. He could understand that but he couldn't understand David's face.

When the ceremony was over, noise and lights and excitement exploded over Joe and the other graduates.

Ellie got more pictures and a kiss which embarrassed her.

"Joe! You're not supposed to kiss like that in front of people!" she said, and handed him a small box wrapped in dark-brown satin. Inside was a poem in a miniature black-velvet frame:

> To Joe
> I
> wrote
> this
> poem
> to tell you
> of
> my love
> Ellie

Ellie had trouble opening Joe's present because she was sniffling and when she saw the diploma charm and read the inscription, she began to cry. Joe had to wipe her nose before he could open Phil's present.

"Ellie called me and told me about the Navy thing," Phil said, laughing. "So I figured you could use these."

When Joe opened the green box and saw the photographs he put the lid back on as fast as he could, grinning at Phil and looking quickly at Ellie and his aunt beside him.

But the old woman in the draped black dress said nothing, just hugged him.

Then David gave him a handmade cream-colored dashiki and pulled him aside.

Before David could say anything, Aunt Lou reached up and put her wrinkled fingers against his lips. David looked uncomfortable but he did not move.

Aunt Lou's face looked terrible.

She took her fingers away, and began to mumble. Joe thought she would scream, but she didn't and he was glad.

"Joey," David said.

It was then that Aunt Lou screamed. Ellie saw her twisted mouth and put her arms around her. Joe wanted to do something but he wasn't sure what. More important now was the way his brother looked.

"Davey, what's the matter? You been looking funny all night."

"Wait!" Aunt Lou was opening the little black pouch. "This got my whole life in it," she said, trembling.

Joe saw people beginning to gather around them. Then he heard David's voice.

"Paul found the money," David said. "The money's gone."

13

"He was coming here with me to see you graduate and he put on that old jacket to wear, where you hid the money. I tried to get him to wear something else, but by that time he had put his hand in the pocket and found it."

Joe felt as though he were enclosed in ice. Through it, he heard his aunt's voice.

"It done," she said.

Joe was still standing there when Phil started moving. "Let's go, baby," he said to Joe. "Maybe we can get him before he gives it up."

Joe came together quickly. "Davey," he said, half running behind Phil, who was moving fast toward the auditorium doors, "take Aunt Lou and Ellie home."

"Joe, I'm scared," Ellie cried. "Don't go!"

"That money's got a job to do, Ellie," Joe said.

David was running along beside Joe. "I'm going with you, Joey," he said.

"You can't handle this, Davey. Go home. Get Aunt Lou and Ellie out of here."

"I'm coming with you."

"*I said go home!*"

David was still there. Joe grabbed him and rammed him hard against an aisle seat. David stumbled backward. Someone was pulling Joe away but he held tight to David. "I said go *home!*"

Phil hollered, "We're losing time, baby."

Joe reached into his pocket, grabbed some money, and stuffed it into David's hand. "Go home!" he said and ran after Phil.

"You stay out of this, Phil," Joe said. "If I can't get Paul or if he ain't got it—I'm going all the way to Warwick. I'm getting Davey's money back."

"You got me with you then," Phil said. "What happens to you happens to me."

Phil saw Paul first. They both knew it was too late, but Joe searched Paul's pockets and socks and shirt and shoes anyway. The pants pockets were torn open.

The money was gone.

Joe grabbed his brother and slammed him against the frame of a metal doorway. "I ought to kill you," he cried. "Kill you!"

But Paul was in a deep nod. Somewhere where nobody but him could go.

Phil shook Paul violently. "Where's the money, man. Open them eyes and see me. Where's the money?"

119

But it was no use. Joe looked at his brother one more time. Then he walked away and didn't look back. If he had, he would have seen Paul lean all the way down and fall.

Joe and Phil were running again. Toward K Street this time. And Warwick.

"We need a gun," Phil said.

"No, Phil. All I want is Davey's money back."

"What we need is a gun," Phil said again.

"Then pretend we got one."

"O.K., but let's cool it, man," Phil said, "and walk. The cops see us, we get detained. They don't believe in black folks jogging."

They knew Warwick was in the K Street record shop when they saw his boys standing outside. The boys saw them coming and one left to go inside. "You see that, Phil—the fat one. The fat one's telling Warwick we here. I got a feeling the money's good."

"Your money's gone—we just here on principle."

"I think the money's good," Joe repeated.

"Been a long time since we rumbled, knocked some heads. How you feel? We getting close."

"Straight, Phil. I feel good."

"Then let's do it like we used to do it. Before we turned good and ruined ourselves."

Joe started grinning. "Phil," he said. "You ready?"

Phil grinned too and snapped his fingers. "Ready, baby. Just like the movies." Clowning with each other, they walked up to the eight boys leaning against the plate glass window. The fat one was back.

"Hey, Brooks," a boy near the end of the line called. "Somebody in your family musta hit the numbers!"

Joe's stomach felt cold. But the coldness was strength. He kept smiling when he spoke. "Which one you chicken monkeys going to tell Warwick I want to see him?"

Some of the boys laughed.

Quietly, and still smiling, Joe spoke again. "Let's see how good you are one at a time. I'll take the first four. Since it was my money and my brother. Then if you still can't get Warwick, Phil will take the other four. One-to-one. You use whatever you got on you. We use what we got on us."

There was silence.

"Who's first?"

Nobody moved.

"If this is the way I have to see Warwick, let it be."

One boy stepped out, or tried to. Joe's foot shot out swift and low, and the boy lay where he had fallen.

"*One!*" Phil yelled. His hand was under his jacket.

Joe fought two more before everything happened. He was fighting the third when another one jumped in and hit him. In a second Phil was beside him. Things were moving well when Joe heard Ellie screaming and police sirens. And David's voice.

"Davey! Get away! Get the hell out of here! I'll beat your ass if you don't get away from me!"

121

But David was doing all right. He was on top of the boy Joe'd been fighting, and Joe was proud of the way he was handling himself. He was moving in to help David when he heard the shot.

He turned and saw that two of Warwick's boys had guns. There were two more shots, and Joe saw the police taking cover.

But there was another boy with a gun, and he was not shooting wild. He was taking dead aim. At Joe. And there was no one near him, or near Joe.

Joe saw that it was the boy he had hit in the stomach the other day. "You mine, Brooks," he yelled.

Joe saw the cops moving in, and wondered, in a split second, if they could take the boy fast enough.

Joe was hit at the same time he heard the shot. The thing that hit him was David.

And the bullet hit David.

Joe leaped for the boy. Hit him, choked him, kicked him.

The policeman, who knew Joe and David, held back and let Joe do what he had to do. Except kill the boy.

Joe felt surrounded and he wanted to get away to his brother.

Ellie was there close. "Don't look, Joe," she cried. "Don't look."

14

Joe knelt down on the sidewalk beside his brother. He knew it was over. The wound had laid open the side of David's head.

Noise was everywhere, but Joe couldn't hear it. An ambulance siren was far off and coming closer, but he couldn't hear that either.

It didn't matter. He wasn't waiting for it. And neither was Davey.

Joe pulled his brother's jacket sleeve down a little. "Your arms are too long, Davey. They're always sticking out of things. But they come on right when you got a ball in your hand. Then, man, you got some pretty arms. Prettiest ones on a basketball court—anybody's court!

"But why you like to study so much? Night and day—just learning things. I could never get it easy as you could. I could get it a little, I guess. But not like you. Not easy." Joe smoothed his brother's collar. "Davey and the books."

The ambulance attendants were trying to put something over David's body but Joe wouldn't let them pull it over his face. "Can't you see I'm talking to him!"

The attendants moved away and Joe stretched out flat beside his brother and kissed him.

"Told you, Davey. People always doing wrong things, messing up. Even loving the wrong people. It wasn't a good place for you. You did everything too good. And that always means trouble." Joe leaned up and looked at David. "How you like Pop last night, Davey? Wasn't that something? He came on good, got hisself together. But I don't know about Momma and Paul. It's hard to tell about them."

Joe stretched out flat again and smiled. "Me? I'll make it, man. I'll make it for you—I promise you, Davey. Wherever I go, you'll be there too. When I do good things, you be doing them with me. In fact, if I do good at all— it'll be 'cause you there with me, man. Yeah, I know it sounds simple, but that's the way it's going to be."

Joe turned away from his brother for a moment to look at Ellie kneeling on the ground beside him. He turned back to David. "When Ellie and me get married and have some kids, I'm going to name my tallest and smartest son after you. I won't name none of them until they all get here and I can figure out which one that is."

Joe started crying. Then he stopped, and put his face against David. "Hey, Davey," Joe said, his voice barely a whisper. "Hey, man—let me tell you 'bout a place." Joe tried to get his face even closer to his brother's, and Ellie, watching him, moved closer to Joe. "Yeah," Joe was saying, "I know. I know you don't dig my stories no more 'cause you think you too big—but you going to hear this one."

Ellie put her hand on Joe's trembling shoulder. He was crying hard.

"You'll like it, man. Everything is real good there, Davey—good like you. Nobody got to worry and fight and stuff like that. The people are together, and trouble never comes. All the mothers love you and tell you, Davey. I swear, man. And all the fathers are strong. The sisters are pretty. And the brothers help each other. It's a love place. A real black love place." Joe tried to smile and couldn't. "I wouldn't kid you, Davey. Only the smart ones get to go—people like you. The good ones."

Joe felt like he was choking. Some giant thing was closing his throat. He reached for Ellie's hand and held it tight. Then he lay closer to his brother's body and hugged it hard. He kissed David's face and tried to hold it, made a fist and brought it gently to his brother's face. Then he reached back and pulled the heavy white cover, put it lightly over David's face. Strong hands were coming from somewhere now, pulling him up. But Joe held tight to David, buried his face on his brother's chest. He didn't know he was yelling.

"Good luck, Davey," he cried. "Good luck, man."

ABOUT THE AUTHOR

SHARON BELL MATHIS was born in Atlantic City, New Jersey, and grew up in Brooklyn's Bedford-Stuyvesant. She and her husband and three daughters, Sherie, Stacy, and Stephanie, now live in Washington, D.C., where she teaches math in a special-education program at Charles Hart Junior High School. She is a staff member of the D.C. Black Writers' Workshop, where she coordinates and teaches the writing of children's literature.

Her first book for Viking, *Sidewalk Story,* was the 1970 winner in its age category of the Council on Interracial Books for Children award. About the writing of *Teacup Full of Roses,* she says, "It's another salute to black kids."